The BIG Book of Berenstain Bears Beginner Books

The BIG Book of *Berenstain Bears* Beginner Books

by **Stan and Jan Berenstain**

Random House · New York

Visit us on the Web!
www.randomhouse.com/kids
berenstainbears.com

Educators and librarians, for a variety of teaching tools, visit us at www.randomhouse.com/teachers

ISBN: 978-0-375-87366-9
Library of Congress Control Number: 2010933949

Printed in the United States of America

30 29 28 27 26 25

First Edition

Contents

The BIG Book of Berenstain Bears Beginner Books

The Bike Lesson

by
Stan and Jan Berenstain

Come here, Small Bear.
Here is something
you will like.

Look, Ma, look!
A brand-new bike.

Thanks, Dad! Thanks!
For me, you say?
I am going to ride it
right away!

Not yet, not yet,

not yet, my son . . .

First come the lessons,

then the fun.

How to get on is

lesson one.

15

Lesson one?

Is that lesson one?

Yes.

That is what

you should not do.

So let that be a

lesson to you.

Yes it was, Dad.

Now I see.

That was a very good
lesson for me.

Dad! Where are you going?
You showed me how.
Why don't you let me
ride it now?

Not yet. Not yet.
Before you do
I'll have to give you
lesson two.

Just watch, Small Bear.
Just watch your Pop.
Lesson two is
how to stop.

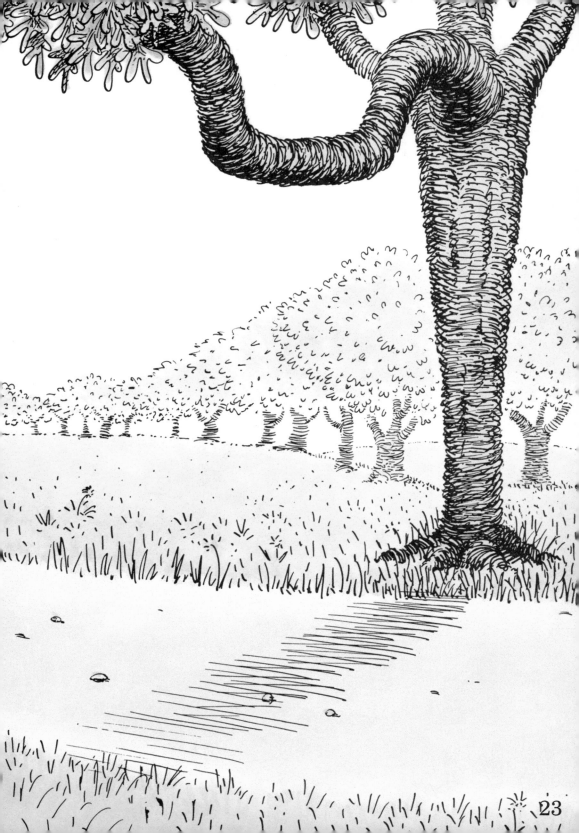

A very good lesson.
Thank you, Pop.

May I ride it now
that you showed me how?
May I?
May I ride it now?

Not yet. Not yet.
You have more to learn.
I'll have to show you
how to turn.

Just watch me . . .

28

This is lesson
number three.

Wow! What a lesson!
That number three!
That may be a little
too hard for me.

This is what
you must never do.
Now let this be
a lesson to you.

It surely was, Dad!

Now I see.

That was a very good

lesson for me.

When I get you down
may I ride it then?
May I? May I?
Just say when.

Wait, my son.

You must learn some more.

I have yet to teach

you lesson four.

When you come to a puddle
what will you do?
Will you go around
or ride right through?

It's not so good

to ride right through.

You're right, Dad.
I can clearly see
why that lesson
was good for me.

When I get you out,

may I ride it then?

Please, Dad . . .

Will you tell me when?

Of course. You may ride it.
You can. You will.

. . . After lesson five.

How to go down hill.

Wow! What a lesson!
That looks hard,
going down hill
through a chicken yard.

44

Dad, please tell me . . . will I
ever get to ride it?
Or will I just keep
running beside it?

Pretty soon, Son.

But not just yet.

There is still one lesson

you have to get.

Lesson six is

the hardest yet.

To be a good rider,
to really know how,
you will have to learn
about safety now.

51

To be safe, Small Bear,
when you ride a bike,
you can not just take
any road you like.

Before you take one
you must know . . .

. . . where that road
is going to go.

See?
This is what
you should not do.
Now let this be
a lesson to you.

It surely was, Dad.

Now I see.

That was another good

lesson for me.

May I ride it now?

May I ride it now?

After one more lesson.

It will be the last.

There is one more thing.

I can teach it fast.

When I ride on a road
I take great pride
in always riding
on the right hand side.

But, Dad!

Are you riding

on the right hand side?

I guess I know
my hands, Small Bear.
My right is here.
My left is there.

Or am I wrong?

Now could that be?

Left hand . . . ? Right hand . . . ?

Let me see . . .

Left hand on the
left hand side . . .
Right hand on the
right hand side.

Thank you, Pop!

You showed me how.

But, please

please

PLEASE

may I ride it now?

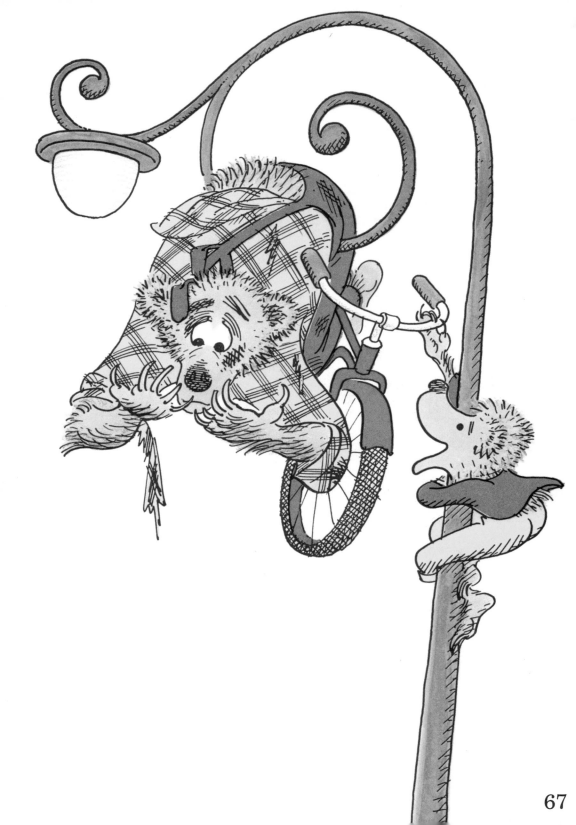

Look, Ma!

Now I can ride it!

See!

Dad had some very good
lessons for me.

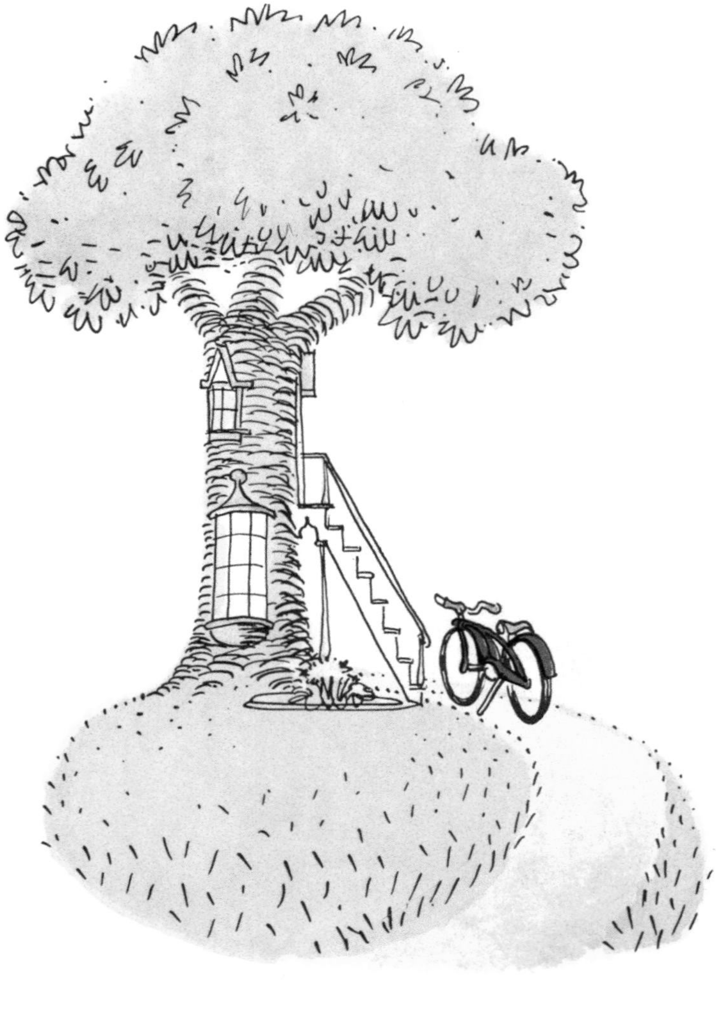

The Bears'
PICNIC

by Stan and Jan Berenstain

Mother Bear,
put your apron away.
We are going to go
on a picnic today!

Where are we going
on our picnic, Dad?

To the very best place
in the world, my lad!

Now you remember
this spot, my dear.
When we were young,
we picnicked here.

Papa, I do not
like to complain,
but your wonderful spot
is next to a train!

Where are we going
now, Papa Bear?
Is there another
wonderful spot somewhere?

Don't pester me
with questions, please.
There's a place I know
right in those trees.

It is everything
a picnic spot should be.
And no one remembers
it is here but me.

What a spot! What a spot!
So quiet! So cool!
Just as it was
when I was in school.

We had a school picnic
and I won first place
for eating the most pie
in a pie-eating race.

Pop, this spot may
be very fine,
but look what it says
on that big sign!

BIG PICNIC TODAY

PICNIC

Dad,
can you find us
another spot?
Are we having
a picnic
today, or not?

Now stop asking questions!
Be quiet! Stop stewing!
Your father knows
what he is doing.

To pick a spot that is
just the right one,
you have to be very
choosy, my son.

Nothing can bother
our picnic here!
Lay out the picnic
things, my dear.

I do not like
to say so, Dad,
but another good spot
has just gone bad.

97

I hope there's another
good spot you know.
But how much farther
do we have to go?

Why don't you use
your eyes, Small Bear?
There's a perfect place
right over there!

The grass is green.

The air is sweet.

Lay out the lunch,

and take a seat.

Hooray!

At last

we're going to eat!

Well . . .

this place is good.

I wasn't wrong.

But I know one better.

Let's move along.

105

106

Now take this perfect
piece of ground.
No one but us
for miles around!

Pop, you picked
the best spot yet.
But how can we picnic
with that jet?

I am very
hungry, Pop!
When is this spot-picking
going to stop?

I am getting tired.

My feet hurt, too.

Any old spot here

ought to do.

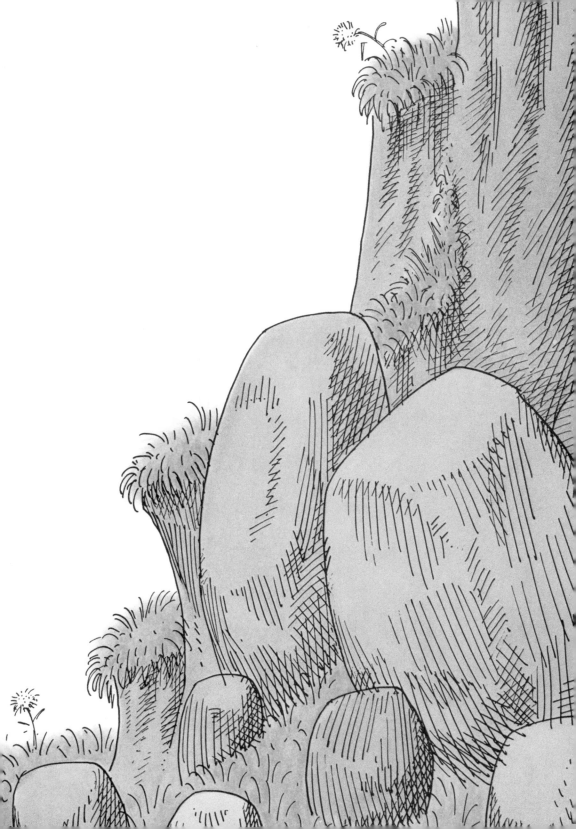

Please, Pop, please,

can't we picnic soon?

It's long past lunch.

It's afternoon!

You have to be choosy,

Pop, I know.

But what's better up here

than down below?

What's up here? . . .
I'll tell you what.
The world's most perfect
picnic spot!

As you can see,
it is perfectly clear
that *nothing* can bother
our picnic here.

No noisy crowds!
No pesky planes!
And no mosquitoes,
trucks or trains!

Oh-oh, Dad.

Here come the rains!

Pooh!
Rain to a bear
is nothing at all.
We'll picnic here
and let it fall.

Come back!

What kind of bears are you?

Scared of a drop

of rain or two!

Bring back that food!

This place will do.

It's dry in here.

It's warm here, too!

It does look warm.

Yes, I agree.

But it looks much, much
too warm for me!

Wait, now! Wait!

You wait for me!

I'll find a better spot.

You'll see.

I'll find the perfect
place to eat.
I'll find a spot
that can't be beat!
The finest spot
you've ever seen. . . .

Now,

THAT

is the kind

of place I mean!

He did it,
Mother.
Did he not?
He found the perfect
picnic spot!

THE BEARS' VACATION

By Stan and Jan Berenstain

Hooray! Hooray!
We're on our way!
Our summer vacation
starts today!

And here we are.

What a wonderful trip!

Let's get in the water!

Let's go for a dip!

Small Bear! Small Bear!

Don't you go too far.

I want to see you

wherever you are.

Don't you worry.

Don't you fear.

I'll show him

all the dangers here.

I'm watching, Dad!

I'm all set to go!

Then here is the first rule
you should know.
Obey all warning signs!
Look around.
Are there any warning signs
to be found?

There is one.
And I think
you should know
it says in big letters,
STRONG UNDERTOW!

Ah, yes, Small Bear.

You're right! It does!

Do you see how good

my first rule was?

Yes, Papa! Here!

Catch hold of this line.

I'll be safe when I swim now.

That lesson was fine.

You will be safe
when diving, too,
after I give you
rule number two.

Look first. Then dive
when all is clear.
Now let's take a look.
Is there anything near?

153

Yes, Dad, there is.

I see a twig!

Never mind that!

It's not very big.

You proved it, Dad.

Even a twig

can be bad.

Right, my son.

That is very true.

It's a pleasure to teach

these rules to you.

Dad, I'll remember

the rules you gave.

Now let's go surfing.

Let's ride on a wave.

Now we go on
to rule number three.
Beware of all rocks
when surfing at sea.

Look, Papa! Rocks!
Right there ahead!
We should beware of them
as you said.

Those rocks are much
too far away.
The surf will not
reach those rocks today.

Then, on the other hand,
we might
end up on those rocks.
You see? I was right!

I think I understand
safety now.
Thank you, Dad,
for showing me how!

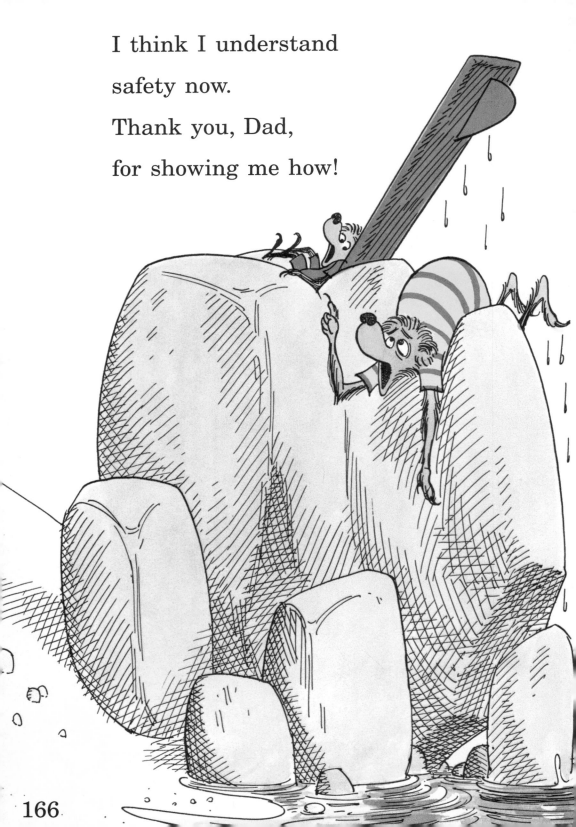

But I have much more
to tell you, my son.
My safety rules
have only begun!

When people vacation
at the shore,
they like to take walks.
They like to explore.

So watch your step
is rule number four.
There are many sharp shells
along the shore.

Here's a sharp one!
I'll step with care.
But may I keep it?
It looks quite rare.

Wait now! Don't touch
anything yet!
There's another rule
you have to get!

Here it is . . .

rule number five.

Watch what you touch.

It may be alive!

Rules four and five
are good to know.
Now I'll be safe
wherever I go.

Not quite, my son.

Hop into this boat!

You must learn the rule

for safety afloat!

Out in a boat,

you must take care.

And here is rule number six,

Small Bear.

Keep a sharp lookout!

It's easy to do.

Watch me, now!

I'll do it for you!

See? Like this!
Only a fool
would sail on the sea
without this rule!

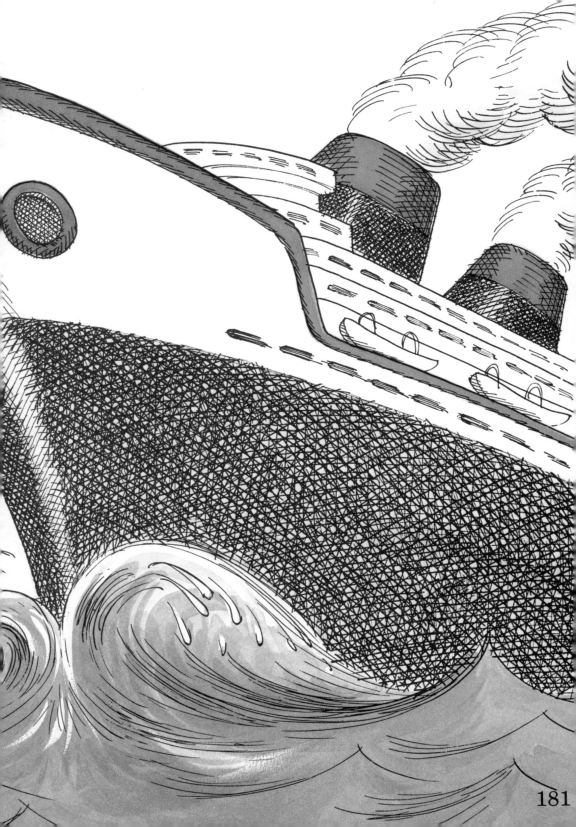

181

It's a very good rule.
I can see that, Dad.
Without it, things might
get very bad!

I've been happy to learn
all you had to teach.
Are we ready, now,
to go back to the beach?

I have one rule more
before we go,
and then you'll know
all you need to know.

One more thing
people do at the shore . . .
they go underwater
and explore.

In exploring
underwater places,
there are many, many
dangerous spaces.

And my last rule
is simple and clear:
Stay out of caves
when exploring down here!

Hmmm. This cave
is big and wide!
It might be safe
to go inside.

As I was saying,
stay out of small spaces,
and any other
dangerous places!

WOW!

We learned that rule
very fast!

195

Tell me, Dad,

was that the last?

Yes, that rule
was the very last one.
My safe vacation rules
are done!

Ma!
You won't have to worry
any more!
Pa taught me how
to be safe at the shore!

BEARS IN THE NIGHT

by Stan and Jan Berenstain

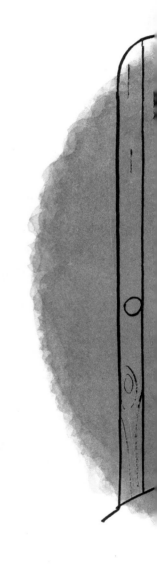

In bed

Out of bed

Out of bed

To the window

At the window

Out the window

Out the window

Down the tree

211

Out the window

Down the tree

Over the wall

Over the wall

Under the bridge

Under the bridge

Around the lake

Under the bridge

Around the lake

Between the rocks

Out the window

Down the tree

Over the wall

Under the bridge

Around the lake

Between the rocks

Through the woods

Up
Spook
Hill!

Down Spook Hill
Through the woods
Between the rocks
Around the lake
Under the bridge
Over the wall
Up the tree . . .

In the window!

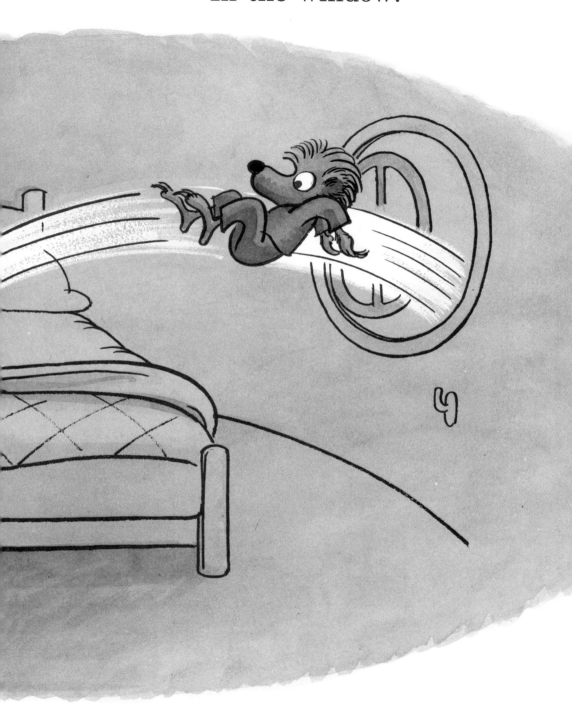

Back in bed

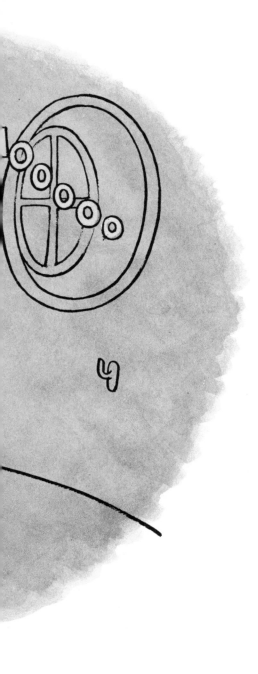

THE BERENSTAIN BEARS
AND THE
SPOOKY OLD TREE

Stan and Jan Berenstain

Three little bears.

One with a light.
One with a stick.
One with a rope.

A spooky old tree.

Do they dare go into
that spooky old tree?

Yes.

They dare.

Three little bears . . .
One with a light.
One with a stick.
One with a rope.

A twisty old stair.

Do they dare go up
that twisty old stair?

Yes.

They dare.

Three little bears.

One with a light.

One with a stick.

And <u>one</u> with the shivers.

A giant key.

A moving wall.

Will the three little bears
go through that wall?
Do they dare go into
that spooky old hall?

Yes.

They dare.

258

Three little bears.
One with a light.
And <u>two</u> with the shivers.

Great Sleeping Bear.

Do they dare go over
Great Sleeping Bear?

Do they dare?
Well . . .

They came into the tree.

They climbed the stair.

They went through the wall . . .

and into the hall.

So of course they went over
Great Sleeping Bear!

Three little bears . . .
without a light,
without a stick,
without a rope.
And <u>all</u> with the shivers!

How will they ever
get out of there?

Three little bears
running fast.

273

Home again.

Safe at last.

The Berenstain Bears and the Missing DINOSAUR

Stan & Jan Berenstain

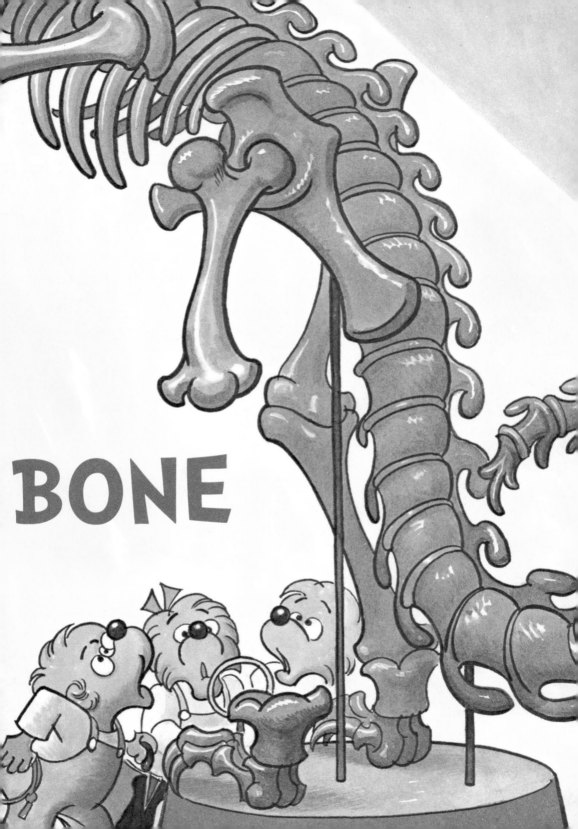

BONE

Bears lining up

outside the door.

Dr. Bear, inside,

pacing the floor.

What's wrong in there?

What's up? What's up?

wonder three little bears

and one little pup.

281

A dinosaur bone
is missing in there!
"Somebody took it!"
said Dr. Bear.
"Who took that bone?
Who took it? Where?"

Three little bears
and their hound dog, Snuff,
come inside
with their detective stuff.

There's no case too hard,
no case too tough,
for the Bear Detectives
and their hound dog, Snuff!

The search begins!
And none too soon.
The Bear Museum
opens at noon.

They will search the place.

Every cranny and nook.

Will they find the bone?

Will they find the crook?

A dark, dark room.

A mummy's tomb!

Is that the thief?

That spooky face?

The MUMMY ROOM

No.

That's the museum's

mummy case.

The Mummy Case of
KING GRIZZLYTUT

Eleven fifteen.

Time grows short.

Now, where would one hide
a bone of that sort?

It could be there,
inside that vase.
The bone thief's
perfect hiding place!

VALUABLE VASE

"You can look
in that valuable vase
if you must.
There's nothing
in there
but some valuable dust."

Not much time left.
Just half an hour!
The Bear Detectives
search the tower.

There he is! The thief!
And the bone he stole!

Wrong again.
That's an
Indian totem pole.

301

It's getting late
but still they look.
And still no bone,
and still no crook.

"Say . . .

maybe bone thieves work in packs.

Three thieves!

With a sword, and a gun, and an ax!"

They had better find
that leg bone soon.
There's just one minute
left till noon!

With no more time
to search and look,
they know they will not
catch that crook.

They failed!
This case is much too hard. . . .

Wait! . . .

What's that out there

in the yard?

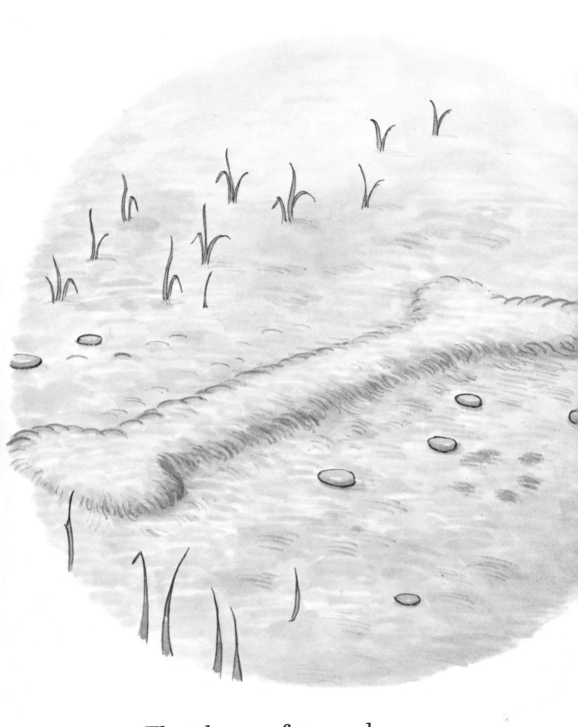

That lump of ground—
that bone-shaped mound!

The missing bone!

It's found! It's found!

With hound dog paw prints
all around.

THE CASE IS SOLVED!

No job's too hard,
no case too tough,
for the Bear Detectives . . .

and that

bone thief, Snuff.

Stan & Jan Berenstain

began writing and illustrating books for children in the early 1960s, when their two sons, Michael and Leo, were young readers themselves. They lived on a hillside in Bucks County, Pennsylvania, a place that still looks a lot like Bear Country. They could see deer, wild turkeys, rabbits, squirrels, and woodchucks through their studio window almost every day—but no bears. The Bears lived inside their hearts and minds.

The Berenstains' sons are all grown up now. Michael is an illustrator and author who works with his mother, Jan, on creating new Berenstain Bears books. Stan and Jan have four grandchildren. Some of them can even draw pretty good bears. With more than two hundred books in print, along with videos, television shows, and even Berenstain Bears exhibits at major museums, it's hard to tell where the Bears end and the Berenstains begin!

BEGINNER BOOKS
by the Berenstains

The Bear Detectives
The Bears' Picnic
The Bears' Vacation
The Berenstain Bears and the Missing Dinosaur Bone
The Big Honey Hunt

BRIGHT & EARLY BOOKS
by the Berenstains

Bears in the Night
The Berenstain Bears and the Spooky Old Tree
The Bike Lesson
Inside, Outside, Upside Down
Old Hat, New Hat